Points of
VIEW

·C·R·I·M·E· ·A·N·D· ·P·U·N·I·S·H·M·E·N·T·

David Pead

Wayland

Points of View

F

Abortion
Advertising
Alcohol
Animal Rights
Censorship
Crime and Punishment
Divorce
Drugs

Medical Ethics
Northern Ireland
Nuclear Weapons
Pollution
Racism
Sex and Sexuality
Smoking
Terrorism

Acknowledgements

The author would like to thank the following for their help: Sue King, Librarian of the Bramshill Police Staff College; David Knowles.

The publishers have attempted to contact all copyright holders of the quotations in this title, and apologize if there have been any oversights.

The publishers gratefully acknowledge permission from the following to reproduce extracts from copyright material:

WH Allen, *The New Murderer's Who's Who* by JHH Gaute and Robin Odell, 1989; Allen and Unwin, article from the Annual Report of the New South Wales Prisons Department 1892-3, *The Failure of Imprisonment: An Australian Perspective* by Roman Tomasic and Ian Dobinson, 1979; Basic Books, *Thinking About Crime* by James Q Wilson, 1975; *Brick of Shame: Britain's Prisons* by Vivien Stem, 1989; *Daily Telegraph*, article by Judge Stephen Tumm, 10 April 1990; Harrap, *Executioner: Pierrepoint* by Albert Pierrepoint, 1974; AM Heath & Co, *1984* by George Orwell, 1949; Heinemann Educational, *Delinquency: Its Roots, Careers and Prospects* by DJ West, 1982; Controller of Her Majesty's Stationery Office, *Crime and Accountability: Victim/Offender Mediation in Practice* by Tony F Marshall and Susan Merry, 1990; Holt Rinehart and Winston, *Crime and Criminology* by Sue Titus Reid, 1988 (fifth ed.); International Association of Chiefs of Police, article by Col. RL Suthard 'What is an AFIS?', *Police Chief*, June 1989; Macmillan, *Crime in America* by Ramsey Clark, 1970; New York University Press, *Compulsive Killers: The Story of Modern Multiple Murder* by Elliot Leyton, 1986; North Eastern University Press, *Legal Homicide: Death as Punishment in America 1864/1982* by William J Bowers, Glenn L Pierce and John F McDevitt, 1974; *Perspectives on Crime Victims*, article by Leroy L Lamborn (eds. Burt Galway and Joe Hudson), 1981; Police Review Publishing Co, 1) *Police Review*, article 'Three Views of Death' by George Whitcombe, 3 April 1987; 2) *Police Review Editorial*, 4 March 1988; 'Policing into the 1990s' *Beyond the Barriers Towards 2000* AD by David A Leonard; Routledge, 1) *Other Cultures* by John Beattie, 1964; 2) *Terrorism and Guerrilla Warfare* by Richard Clutterbuck, 1990; Sage Publications, article by Wesley K Skogan 'Social Change and the Future of Violent Crime', *Violence in America*, vol 1, 1989; Social Development Associates, *Victim Compensation* by Alan T Hartland, 1981; Theron Raines, *Crime Pays* by Thomas Plate, 1975; *Violent Delinquents* by Paul A Strasburg, 1978; George Weidenfeld and Nicolson, *Encyclopaedia of Murder* by Patricia Pitman and Colin Wilson, 1984; John Wiley and Sons, *Handbook of Juvenile Delinquency* by Prof. Arnold Binder (ed. Herbert C Quay), 1987.

Front cover: *Rick Rowe was imprisoned for murder. Whilst in prison, he ran a 'scare campaign', emphasizing the horrors of prison life. It was aimed at preventing young people from turning to crime.*

Consultant: John L. Pottenger Jr., Professor of Law, Yale University, Newhaven, USA

Series Editor: William Wharfe
Editors: Paul Mason/Elizabeth Spiers
Designer: David Armitage

First published in 1991 by
Wayland (Publishers) Limited
61 Western Road, Hove
East Sussex BN3 1JD, England

British Library Cataloguing in Publication Data
Pead, David
    Crime and punishment.
    1. Crime and punishment
    I. Title   II. Series
    364

ISBN 0-7502-0151-7

Phototypeset by Direct Image Photosetting Ltd,
Hove, East Sussex, England
Printed in Italy by G. Canale & C.S.pA, Turin
Bound in France by AG.M.

Contents

1 Introduction

> The only alternative to order is chaos. To maintain an orderly system of social relations people . . . cannot, all the time, do exactly as they like. Often self-interest may (lead to) behaviour incompatible with the common good . . . in every society some rules, some kinds of constraint on people's behaviour, are acknowledged. (John Beattie, *Other Cultures*, 1964.)

Since the earliest times, people have had to work together to survive. In the past they would gather together to find food and make shelter. But a group can only do this if it has rules that most members of the group agree on. If any member of the group disagrees with the rules and will not obey them, that person cannot remain a member of the group. If the member breaks the rules and harms another member of the group, he or she is punished.

Putting someone in the stocks was a common form of punishment in the eighteenth century. Throughout history, people have always been punished for breaking society's rules.

Leicester Prison, England. Imprisonment is the most common form of punishment for criminals today.

Some of the earliest laws are recorded in the Old Testament. As well as the Ten Commandments, many crimes and the punishments for them are set out. 'An eye for an eye, a tooth for a tooth,' comes from there.

Nowadays we live in extremely complex societies made up of millions of people. Laws governing our behaviour are made by governments and cover nearly every aspect of our lives.

> Law is important because it touches virtually every area of human interaction. Law is used to protect ownership, to define the parameters of private and public property, to regulate business, to raise revenue, and to provide compensation when agreements are broken . . . Laws, particularly criminal laws, not only protect private and public interests but also preserve order. Society determines that some interests are so important that a formal system of control is necessary to preserve them; therefore laws must be passed to give the state the power of enforcement. (Sue Titus Reid, *Crime and Criminology*, 1988.)

A crime is an act that is prohibited by law. This can be anything from stealing money to killing another human being. Society has said, through its laws, that such acts threaten the stability of the community and are therefore not allowed.

But individuals do commit crimes. So the law goes one step further, and says that such crimes will be punished. On the whole, criminals are fined or put in prison as punishment for their actions.

Everyone agrees that acts such as murder and rape are crimes and deserve punishment. But our idea of what constitutes a crime does sometimes change. In the Old Testament one of the laws recorded in Exodus says that 'He that curseth his father, or his mother, shall surely be put to death'. This seems savage to us today and few people would argue that we should still have such a law. However, our ideas of which acts constitute a crime can change day by day.

> A boy in Wisconsin, for example, derives great pleasure from letting air out of the automobile tyres in his neighbourhood. The people in that neighbourhood may, on the one hand, be in a euphoric mood because of a major industrial development in the area and react to the behaviour as an adolescent prank, a minor nuisance worthy of no more than a scolding call to his parents. On the other hand, the community may be tense because of a local or regional crisis, and may react by calling the police and having the boy arrested. (Prof. Arnold Binder, *Handbook of Juvenile Delinquency*, 1987.)

When can I have a drink?
When you can have an alcoholic drink in Australia and what punishment you can expect if you drink too much depends on where you are. In almost every state the legal drinking age limit is eighteen. Some of the punishments for being drunk in public are: Tasmania — A$100 fine or 1 month in prison; South Australia — not punishable by law, but people are taken home or locked up for their own safety; Victoria — A$100 fine or three days in prison for a first offence, A$500 fine or 1 month in prison for a second offence and for three offences in a year, 12 months in prison.

Two policemen making an arrest. The police are responsible for protecting the public against criminals.

If our idea of what constitutes a crime can change, how can we decide what is the appropriate punishment for a crime? How can we make a law that says that if you let down car tyres you will get fined, if sometimes the same act does not even seem to be a crime?

To answer this we have to ask ourselves what the point of punishment is. The crime has already been committed. In the case of someone who has killed another person, putting the killer in prison will not bring the victim back to life. In fact, by taking away the murderer's freedom, society is harming the murderer. Can two wrongs make a right?

Peter Sutcliffe (covered by a blanket), the Yorkshire Ripper, is escorted to a police station for questioning. He was eventually sentenced to life imprisonment for the murders he committed. Does imprisonment mean that he would never again commit murder if he were to be released?

Over the years many people have argued about the moral justification of punishment, and two main theories have arisen. The first justifies punishment on the grounds that by putting a criminal in prison you stop that person from committing another crime. Society has been protected by restricting the criminal's freedom. This theory admits the possibility of stopping crime from being committed in other ways — for example, by making criminals do community service so that they begin to feel valued by society, or by training someone to do a job so that they do not need to steal to make a living.

The second theory is simpler and just says that crime is wrong and criminals deserve to go to prison.

The difference between the two theories is important, because your opinion on what punishment a criminal should suffer depends on which theory you believe in. Should we free a murderer when it can be shown that he or she will not kill again, or should a murderer be set free only when the price has been paid for the crime?

Country	Age for drinking alcohol	Punishment for public drunkenness
Australia	see separate information box on page 6	
New Zealand	20	Police send letter
Norway	Wine & beer 18 Spirits 20	Pay a fine. The amount varies
India	Drinking completely illegal in most places	
Italy	No age limit	Pay a fine
China	No law	
UK	18	May be detained until sober
USA	Usually 21, but varies from state to state	Varies

1 What do the information boxes on the law for drinking tell you about definitions of what is a crime and what is not?
2 Do you agree that everyone should obey laws in which they might not have had a say — for example, laws that were made several hundred years ago?

Two offenders on a community service project, where they are working with the mentally handicapped. This is thought by many to be a good way of stopping reoffending — it is claimed that community service makes criminals feel valued by society.

2

Born criminal?

Why do people commit crimes? In the USA, a country with a very high crime rate, much work has gone into trying to answer this question.

> One day I was having lunch in a typical, dingy New York luncheonette with a contact who makes at least $100,000 a year dealing in illegal drugs. At one point I got up to use the pay phone, which was located about ten feet from the counter. When I got back, I mentioned casually to my contact that not only had I got my dime back but the telephone had returned a quarter as well.
>
> The man bolted up from the soda fountain, ran to the phone booth, and began slamming the side of the phone.
>
> This is the criminal mentality. (Thomas Plate, *Crime Pays*, 1975.)

Of course this kind of behaviour could simply be described as greedy, and there are many greedy people who are not criminals. Criminals may be produced by the society they live in, rather than being born that way.

The jewellery department of London's Selfridges store. Does such a collection of valuable objects, evidence of an abundant consumer society, tempt people to steal, or are thieves 'born' to their crime?

> In every major city in the United States you will find that two thirds of the arrests take place among only about two per cent of the population. Where is that area in every city? Well it's the same place where infant mortality is four times higher than in the city as a whole; where the death rate is twenty-five per cent higher; where life expectancy is ten years shorter; where common communicable diseases with the potential of physical and mental damage are six and eight and ten times more frequent; where alcoholism and drug addiction are . . . [much more common than in] the rest of the city; where education is poorest – the oldest school buildings, the most crowded and turbulent schoolrooms, the fewest certified [qualified] teachers, the highest rate of dropouts; where the average formal schooling is four to six years less than for the city as a whole. (Ramsey Clark, former Attorney General of the USA, *Crime in America*, 1970.)

Crime in the USA

Each year in the 1980s about 20,000 Americans were murdered. Most of them were young men. Each year more than 75,000 women reported attacks by rapists to police. Another half a million people reported robberies, more than 650,000 told police they were the victims of serious non-sexual assault.

According to US Bureau of Justice statistics, in 1984 the murder rate in the USA was five times greater than in Western Europe, with reported rapes six times and robberies four times as common.

A group of young unemployed people. Some people argue that, because they have nothing to do and very little money, these people are more likely to commit crimes of theft.

If you found a way to steal something you wanted without being caught, would you do it?

But do people steal because they are poor? Are all poor people criminals? Although there is more crime in poor neighbourhoods, most people do not steal, whether rich or poor.

> The United States has, on the whole, the most severe set of criminal penalties in its lawbooks of any advanced Western nation; it also has the highest crime rate of advanced Western nations. One reason may be that . . . we have . . . a high level of personal affluence and an abundant consumer economy. A person wishing to drive a fancy car may well conclude that the slight chance of having to pay a heavy penalty should he be caught stealing is more than outweighed by the immediate pleasure he will derive from having the car, a pleasure that he would have to defer for a long time, perhaps indefinitely, if he were content with the low paying jobs available to him. (James Q Wilson, *Thinking About Crime*, 1975.)

3

Prisons: holiday camps or dungeons?

The restriction of an individual's liberty, by the use of prisons, is the most common form of punishment used in the West for offenders found guilty of serious crimes. This has not always been so; up until the eighteenth century the most common punishments were flogging (whipping), the loss of a hand or ear, or death. When the death penalty was abolished the modern prison system began to develop.

> Those who complain that prisoners are not reformed in gaol should remember that prison is not strictly speaking a reformatory. It is a place to which offenders are sent to serve certain periods of time under a stern and exact discipline as a punishment and a warning to others, as well as for the protection of society. (Annual Report of the New South Wales Prisons Department 1892-93, quoted in *The Failure of Imprisonment: An Australian Perspective*, Roman Tomasic & Ian Dobinson, 1979.)

A scene in Newgate Prison, England, over 100 years ago. Conditions in prisons were appalling at this time.

The ideas of 100 years ago are now being questioned. In recent times the emphasis has moved towards trying to reform offenders within the confines of the prison.

> When our attention is somehow drawn to the subject of prison reform, we are prone to demand whether the change will make it too nice or too nasty for the prisoners, too much of a holiday camp or too much of a medieval dungeon. I submit that we should instead be asking a quite different question: is prison training a man (or woman) to learn how to live as a citizen in the community? I tend on inspections to look at a prison as a pre-release course from the moment the prisoner arrives. I look for City and Guild courses in welding or computers, not for mail-bag or prison-shirt sewing. (Judge Stephen Tumim, Her Majesty's Chief Inspector of Prisons, *Daily Telegraph*, 10 April 1990.)

Above *Inmates in an American prison making number plates. Is this type of simple, repetitive task the right preparation for life outside prison?*

Bread or prisons?

The *New York Times* reported in 1989 that state spending on prisons during the 1980s had risen by 14.2 per cent. During the same period, spending on welfare (helping people without enough money to live on) rose by only 4 per cent, far less than the cost of buying food.

Some people think that the whole concept of prisons as an effective way of dealing with crime has failed.

> Does it [prison] stop those who are sent there committing crimes again? Facts and figures in answer to this are straightforward. No, it is not very successful. The majority of people leaving prisons are not so chastened by their ordeal that they refrain from committing more crime. The young especially seem to pay it little heed. Even the average male adult seems prepared to risk it again in many cases. Of those leaving prison in 1984 [in the UK] three out of ten were back inside by 1986. (Vivien Stern, *Brick of Shame; Britain's Prisons*, 1989.)

Below *Alcatraz prison in the USA (closed in 1963) was one of the most hated and notorious prisons in the world. But did the threat of being sent here ever prevent people from committing serious crimes?*

A cell in Dartmoor prison, England. Many people think this type of imprisonment is harmful to prisoners, while others claim that they deserve this type of isolation.

Those who say that prison does nothing to make people give up a life of crime point out that it may actually do them harm. They say that a spell in prison makes it even more likely that people will commit crime.

Crowded prisons

When Ronald Reagan became President of the USA in 1981, he was determined to stop street violence. New laws were created. At the time there were 477 empty beds in federal (i.e. non-state) prisons.

In the ten years since, 1,770 prosecuting lawyers, 1,015 drug agents and 1,740 FBI agents were employed. Less than 2,000 extra jail spaces were made at the same time. Overcrowding is now a major problem in US prisons.

> Common sense suggests that those who are spending all their time, day in, day out, with people all characterised by having broken the law will devote some part of that time to talking about what they have in common, that is, breaking the law. They will probably discuss their successes and failures and dream about doing it more successfully and getting away with it next time. (*Brick of Shame*, 1989.)

Strangeways prison riot, Manchester, UK, 1990. Two prison officers, standing amidst the debris thrown down from the roof by rioting prisoners, attempt to persuade the prisoners to give themselves up.

Prison riots

The UK's prisons are among the oldest and most cramped in the West. In 1990, prisoners at Manchester's Strangeways jail took over the prison. It was the UK's worst prison riot of the century.

Before the riot, prisoners at the jail were often forced to spend up to twenty-three hours every day locked in their cells because of a lack of prison officers to guard them. Cells designed in Victorian days to hold one prisoner were often used to house three. Few cells had any toilet facilities, so prisoners were forced to share a bucket, slopping out once a day.

The minister in the UK responsible for prisons, David Mellor, dismissed suggestions that the rioters were desperate men protesting against inhumane conditions, saying they were 'bad people behaving badly'.

Folsom prison, USA. Here prisoners are allowed to do physical training and to educate themselves for life after prison. Many people think that this is a more positive and better way of treating prisoners.

1   Should prisons be uncomfortable places? Is the restriction of an individual's freedom enough of a deterrent to stop people committing crimes, or should prisoners also be deprived of such things as televisions and sport?
2   What punishments might deter people from committing crimes other than sending them to prison?
3   In Britain, a fifth of the prison population are people who cannot, or will not, pay fines. Is prison the appropriate punishment for such a crime? If not, how else could they be punished?

In 1970, the State of Iowa in the USA abolished its Polk County Jail and started using more 'community-based corrections', such as parole under supervision, probation and community service. At the same time the State of Massachusetts abolished all its juvenile institutions. Reformers claim that while there is little evidence to suggest these innovations reduced the level of crime, the crime rate did not appear to rise.

In West Germany judges reduced the number of young offenders in prison by one-third between 1983 and 1990, and reduced the length of sentences generally by 20 per cent. The declining rate of imprisonment has been accompanied by falling rates for many crimes, including an 8 per cent fall in violent offences between 1983 and 1987.

4

On death row

> I was death on women. I didn't feel they need to exist. I hated them, and I wanted to destroy every one I could find. I was doing a good job of it. I've got [killed] 360 people, I've got 36 states, in three different countries. My victims never knew what was going to happen to them. I've had shootings, knifings, strangulations, beatings, and I've participated in actual crucifixions of humans. All across the country, there's people just like me, who set out to destroy human life. (Henry Lee Lucas, quoted in *Compulsive Killers: The Story of Modern Multiple Murder*, Elliot Leyton, 1986.)

The guillotine was introduced as a form of execution in 1792 during the French Revolution. The last execution by guillotine was in 1977. In 1981 the French government outlawed capital punishment.

Henry Lee Lucas began his murderous career in 1960, when, at the age of 23, he stabbed his mother to death in bed. He then spent the next fifteen years in prisons and mental hospitals in Michigan, USA, without being cured of his desire to kill people. On his release, he spent eight years criss-crossing the continent, looking for women to rape and murder.

The execution by hanging of Dr Crippen, who was found guilty of murdering his wife in 1910. Hanging was abolished in the UK in 1965.

Some people believe that men like Henry Lee Lucas deserve to die, because their crimes are so horrible that society should not allow them to live.

> The problem of capital punishment was solved for me in 1927 when Police Constable Reg Gutteridge was gunned down in a quiet Essex lane after he stopped the driver of a stolen car. As PC Gutteridge lay dying, his killer, Frederick Browne, shot out both his eyes. When Browne and his accomplice, William Kennedy, were hanged who could possibly dispute the rightness of this sentence? To have offered the other cheek to such scoundrels would have been criminal folly. I was only 16 at the time but now, after a lifetime in the police service, I still believe justice was done. (George Whitcombe, *Three Views of Death*, *Police Review*, 3 April 1987.)

But opponents of capital punishment say that taking a human life is so terrible it can never be justified. By sentencing a murderer to death, society is acting in the same way as the murderer.

> Many reputable persons have advanced to me the view that society cannot do without the death penalty. I emphatically disagree. It seems to me obvious that a point will come where the human race will regard all killing as a remnant of the dark ages, and that, if human evolution means anything at all, it means an increased love of life – all life. The word 'evil' has almost no meaning in modern psychological terms. Human acts are stupid or misguided. If evil has a meaning in modern terms, it is insensitivity to the sufferings of others. This kind of insensitivity is the opposite of what we mean by civilization and evolution. (Patricia Pitman and Colin Wilson, *Encyclopaedia of Murder*, 1984.)

Does the knowledge that if you murder someone you will receive the death penalty stop would-be murderers from killing others? Or are most murders committed by people who have not thought what they are doing or what their punishment might be?

> There is a night of drinking . . . A fight begins. Someone picks up a knife or a gun. A body falls, a neighbor screams, the police arrive, the culprit is encountered, still standing with the weapon in his hand, gazing in drunken bewilderment at his victim. (*Thinking about Crime*.)

The cost of death row
Since the turn of the century more than 7,000 people have been executed in the USA. In February 1989 there were 2,151 men, women and juveniles on death row awaiting execution. Each year the numbers on death row increase by about 250, although there are rarely more than 20 executions a year. As the backlog of death sentences grows, the burden on the legal system and the taxpayer rises. Theodore Bundy spent nine years on death row and cost the taxpayer more than US$3 million through his appeals for clemency in the courts.

> During my twenty-five years as executioner, I believed with all my heart that I was carrying out a public duty. I conducted each execution with great care and a clear conscience. I never allowed myself to get involved with the death penalty controversy.

It is said to be a deterrent. I cannot agree. There have been murders since the beginning of time, and we shall go on looking for deterrents until the end of time. It is I who have faced them last, young lads and young girls, working men, grandmothers. I have been amazed to see the courage with which they take that walk into the unknown. It did not deter them then, and it had not deterred them when they committed what they were convicted for. All the men and women whom I have faced at that final moment convince me that in what I have done I have not prevented a single murder. (Albert Pierrepoint, *Executioner: Pierrepoint*, 1974.)

Opponents of the death penalty go even further. They argue that executions teach us that it is right to kill in certain situations. They argue that far from acting as a deterrent, the death penalty may cause more murders.

The gas chamber at San Quentin jail in the USA. Gas chambers were introduced as a form of execution in the state of Nevada, USA, in 1924. The prisoner is strapped to a chair in a sealed chamber. Lethal gas is then pumped into the chamber. If the prisoner breathes deeply, death is almost instantaneous.

When Theodore ('Ted') Bundy was executed in 1989, crowds outside the prison cheered his death. The publicity surrounding this type of event is criticized by some who say that this diminishes the deterrent effect of the death penalty.

> Executions demonstrate that it is correct and appropriate to kill those who have gravely offended us. The fact that such killings are to be performed only by duly appointed officials on duly convicted offenders is a detail that may get obscured by the message that such offenders deserve to die. If the typical murderer is someone who feels that he has been betrayed, dishonored, or disgraced by another person, then it is not hard to imagine that the example executions provide may inspire a potential murderer to kill the person who has greatly offended him. In effect, the message of the execution may be lethal vengeance, not deterrence. (William J Bowers, Glenn L Pierce & John F McDevitt, *Legal Homicide: Death as Punishment in America, 1864/1982*, 1984.)

Many executions attract huge publicity. The drama of the approaching death of a convicted murderer makes compulsive television viewing. When Theodore Bundy was sent to the electric chair in 1989 for the rape and murder of a twelve- year-old girl, crowds turned up outside his prison in Florida, USA, to cheer his death. Some of the crowd wore 'Burn, Bundy, Burn' T-shirts and there were reports of 'Bundy Barbecues' held that day. But newspapers covering his case made many references to his 'film-star good looks' and a film of his life has now been made. Critics say that such publicity turns the event into a media 'circus', and diminishes the deterrent effect of the punishment.

Douglas Hurd, then UK Home Secretary, was booed when he told delegates at the Conservative Party Conference of 1987 that he was against the death penalty.

1   The USA is almost alone among Western nations in exercising the death penalty. Do you think that this shows that the USA is less civilized than other countries?
2   Does the publicity surrounding the execution of a convicted murderer deter other people from committing murders?
3   If we accept the death penalty for murder, should all murders bring the death penalty, or are some murders worse than others?

> What happens, as we see from the United States, or indeed from Malaysia, is that the offender, in a thoroughly perverse way, becomes treated as the victim. His sorrowing family is interviewed, his words and actions become famous, his last moments are lovingly described. I simply do not believe the public would find this acceptable for long. A circus would be created and the holder of my office, because he would still be the guardian of the Prerogative of Mercy [and have the power to pardon criminals], would be cast as the ringmaster.
(Douglas Hurd, UK Home Secretary, during the June 1988 House of Commons debate on capital punishment.)

5

Victims' rights

When a crime has been committed, the criminal justice system rolls into action. Vast amounts of money are spent each year on police officers who catch criminals, courts that judge and sentence them and prisons that carry out the sentences. But what happens to the victim of the crime? She or he has been hurt by the crime itself and the effect can last a long time.

> Victims' support volunteers meet time after time the victims who wait in fear of the return of the supposed ogre who previously invaded their privacy, the victims who cannot walk down the streets without suspecting every neighbour they meet, or the victims who fume with impotent anger over the wickedness of people who cannot possibly 'have any thought for others'. (Tony F Marshall and Susan Merry, *Crime and Accountability: Victim/Offender Mediation in Practice*, 1990.)

Police officers during riot training. Vast amounts of money are spent every year on training the police. Yet little or no government money goes to compensate the victims of crime.

It is often said that victims of crime get forgotten, as the authorities concentrate on catching the criminals.

> The boy was 11 years old when he was murdered. He was attacked and strangled on a common, less than 100 yards from his own house. His parents were devastated, and the local police appalled. The murderer was soon traced, committed, tried and convicted. Some time later, the dead boy's father went to his local police station, asking to see the officer who had been in charge of the case. He had been promoted and transferred.

> Was there anyone else who had been concerned in the investigation available to speak to him? Well, no. The murder team had been disbanded, some officers had moved on, others were involved in new investigations, more recent murders. The case was closed. What did the father want?

> He had only one question. Why had nobody kept in touch with him? A man had admitted the murder of his son, the criminal justice system had processed him efficiently, and the only information the father ever received about these events was contained in eight lines of print alongside a picture of a topless model in the *News of the World*. (*Police Review Editorial*, 4 March 1988.)

In order to help such people, volunteers have joined together into support groups, to help victims of crime come to terms with the trauma they have suffered. Many of the volunteers were victims themselves and can provide practical help as well as sympathy. Although the clock cannot be turned back to wipe away the crime, the victim can be compensated.

> Rather than paying a debt to the victim, the offender now pays his (or her) 'debt to society'. The next appropriate step, it is argued, must be to . . . give the victim the right to collect from society as a whole.

> An alternative approach used to justify compensation as a right of the victim has been to suggest that the state has failed to protect the victim, from whom it takes taxes for law enforcement and corrections. Under this version of the 'rights' argument the victim has been denied the protection due him (or her) and society must assume the responsibility for restoring the status quo. (Alan T Hartland, *Victim Compensation*, 1981.)

Opposite *This young person is recovering in hospital — the victim of a vicious attack. The physical wounds will heal quickly, but the victim will have to live with the mental trauma — maybe for the rest of his life.*

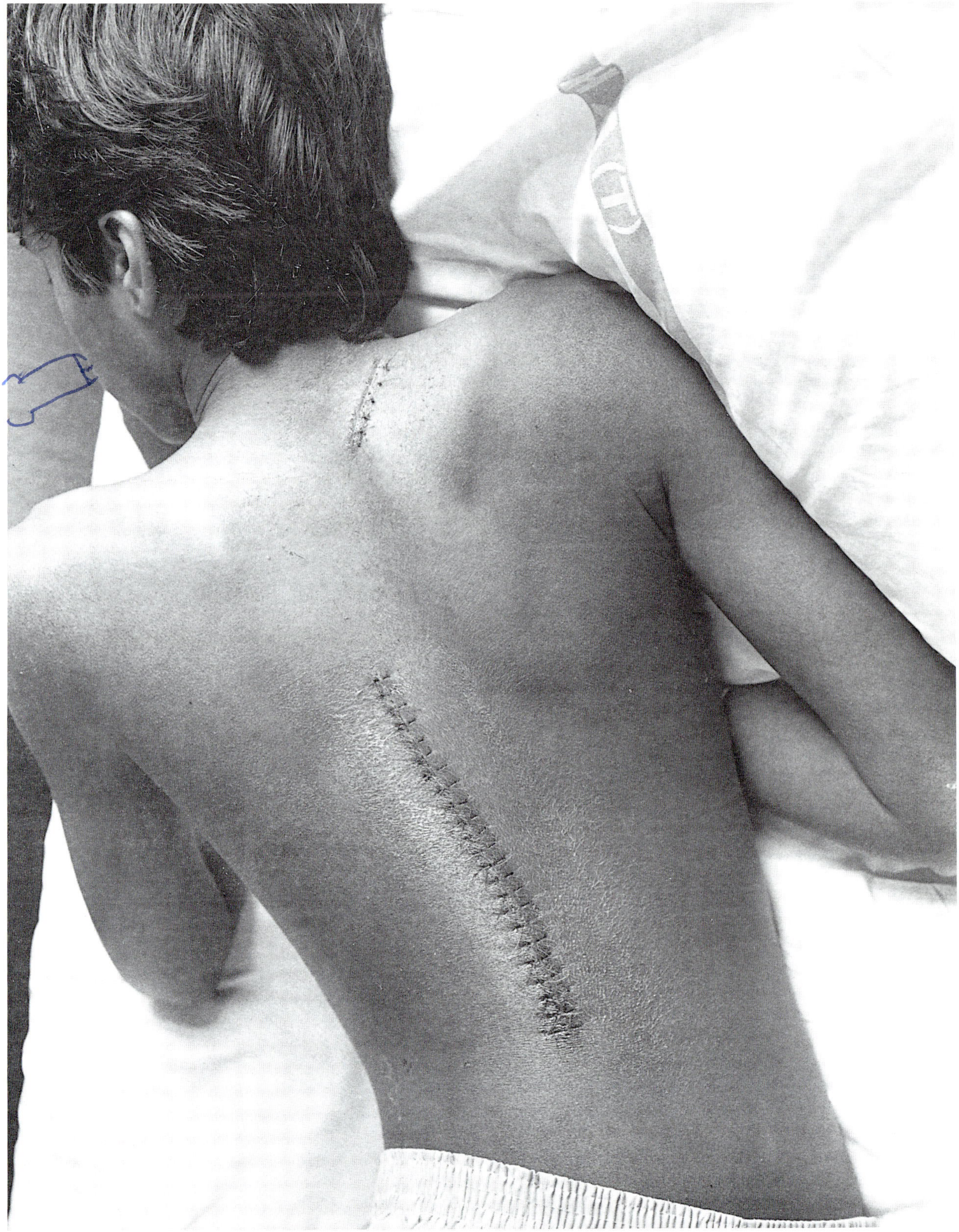

The scene after a burglary. This type of crime often leaves the victims not only materially worse off, but also with feelings of fear and dislike associated with the place where the burglary took place — their own home.

The first crime victim compensation programme, in which money was paid to the victim of a crime by the state, was set up in New Zealand in 1963. Most Western nations now offer payments to victims of crime.

> In the typical [compensation] programme, the person directly injured as a result of a crime of violence is entitled to reimbursement for reasonable hospital and medical expenses and a limited award for income lost because of injuries sustained. If he [or she] dies from his [or her] injuries, his [or her] dependents are entitled to limited awards for funeral and burial expenses and for lost support. With very minor exceptions, the victim receives no award for loss of or damage to property, for injuries received through violations of traffic laws, or pain and suffering . . . the victim deemed partially responsible for the crime receives at most a reduced award, and the victim injured by a close relative usually receives nothing. As a result of all of these limitations on benefits the vast majority of crime victims are not covered by the programmes. (LeRoy L Lamborn, *Perspectives on Crime Victims*, Burt Galway and Joe Hudson (eds.), 1981.)

In the UK £40 million was paid out to victims of crime by the state in 1987. But many of the 45,000 people who applied for money were turned down. One of the problems is that if every victim of a crime were to be paid, taxes would have to be raised. In 1977, the Governor of Indiana, in the USA, vetoed the setting up of a compensation programme because it had been estimated it might cost the state more than US$13 billion.

---

1   Do you agree that society has a responsibility to look after the victims of crime?

2   Should the police and courts have the responsibility for letting victims of crime know what has happened to the criminal in their case? Would such information actually help victims get over the trauma of the crime they have suffered?

3   If you accept that victims of crime should be paid compensation by the state, should money be given to all victims or just those who have suffered the most serious harm?

Car crashes are often caused when one of the drivers is under the influence of alcohol – a criminal offence. It can be difficult to get compensation for injuries or losses sustained as a result of this type of crime.

6

Youth crime

Any consideration of crime would not be complete without looking at the effect of young people on crime statistics. In the UK nearly one-quarter of all known offenders are aged under seventeen, involved mainly in robbery and burglary where they commit about a third of all offences. In the USA the age structure of the population is often used to explain the crime explosion. In 1964, the first of the children born during the post-Second World War 'baby boom' celebrated their sixteenth birthdays. A major rise in crime was reported. In 1966, the President's Crime Commission estimated that between 40 and 50 per cent of the increase in crime over the previous five years was committed by people aged 15-21.

While these figures may show the extent of crime among young people, they do not explain why so many find criminal activity attractive.

Opposite *Newspapers in the UK have highlighted recent cases of crimes committed by teenagers.*

Below *Places where young children like these can play out in the streets and be safe are becoming increasingly rare. Many people have moved away from city centres to the suburbs in recent years, so that their children can grow up away from violence and crime.*

VIOLENT NEW WORLD OF TEENY THUGS

Terror in our cities

By BARRY GARDNER

YOUNG thugs have helped to push crime to epidemic proportions. And police fear the trend will get worse as the year goes on.

THE CITIES yesterday revealed the growing menace of violent young thugs.

IN LONDON — where there has been a terrifying outbreak of brutal attacks on old people — one in every four crimes was committed by a youngster. Of those arrested for robbery 60 per cent were under 21.

When the figures were announced Assistant Commissioner Gilbert Kelland said : " There is very little moral shame when they are arrested. Morality seems to have gone out of the window.

" In my day old people were sacrosanct and could move anywhere any time in London without a finger being laid upon them. That's a reflection of society on all of us."

IN BIRMINGHAM, one murder was believed to [...] [...] charged

Figures released yesterday show that a staggering 2,688,137 crimes were committed in England and Wales in 1980. Children played an increasing role in damage and violence.

And many of them were as young as ten—the minimum age for prosecution.

As the shock report was issued, a Police Federation spokesman firmly laid the blame for teenage offences at the door of unemployment.

" There's bound to be a lot of juvenile delinquency while there are many people out of work," he said.

Gloomier

" I don't think you'll see an improvement until the economy and the jobs situation brighten up."

Sir James Crane, Her [...] Chief Inspector of [...] whose annual [...] —

'The dole is to blame'

of the community, the problem of delinquency among young people needs to be tackled with vigour and determination.

" I subscribe to the view that, above all, standards of behaviour need to be set and control exercised from within the family."

Sir James added that it was "extremely difficult" to identify the reasons for increasing crime.

But, referring to recent riots, [...] out the use of elite [...] to enforce

Wakefield . . . could fall down at any moment

Pentonville . . . the walls are in danger of collapse

Parkhurst . . . needs millions of pounds spending on it

Brixton . . . very seriously decrepit

Crisis as jails crumble away

By MARTIN LINTON

[...] seriously [...] built in [...] paint" or [...] down, [...] report [...] Commons [...] Commit-

[...] less than a [...] programme of [...] ment and re-[...] — costing £1,000m — will [...] from col-

[...] listened in [...] the physical [...]

chief Duncan Buttery warned : " The whole estate is — to put not too exaggerated a view on it — collapsing round our ears.

" It is suffering from years of neglect and needs a massive injection of capital if we're to have prisons standing at the end of the decade."

On top of the modernisation programme, the all party group of MPs called for urgent steps to cut down overcrowding.

Urgent

THE COLD-EYED CHILDREN WHO ATTACK 'FOR FUN'

By PETER KENT
Crime Reporter

IN packs, like wild animals, cold-eyed youngsters roam the stark grey tower blocks of the Silwood Estate.

They don't attack in self-defence, they don't attack to survive. They attack for fun.

Some are just 11 years old.

Said one senior detective last night : " They'd cut a throat for a laugh. They are a nightmare become more and more real as Britain, [...] [...] Silwood [...] have [...] confl[...]

Silwood is merely a microcosm of the malaise creeping insidiously through the fabric of British society.

Latest Gallup [...] show that [...] Britons [...] knif[...]

demanded life sentences for the hoodlums who make life live in fear.

The question [...] was : "[...]

Inquiry into children's home that bred young criminals

Daily Mail Reporter

AN inquiry into a children's home used as a base for drug dealing and prostitution was demanded by Health [...] Virginia Bot-

Sunday newspaper story about the home had made disturbing reading. 'I have asked my officials for an urgent report,' she added. [...] report. Victorian [...] Cam-

sacked for serious misconduct. One had formed a relationship with a girl of 17. The other failed to act when drugs were brought into the home.

Officials admit that finding staff to control teenagers has always been a problem. A Southwark spokesman said last night : [...] been planning to [...] for a year.

smaller, purpose-built accommodation where they can be better supervised.' Until its closure, Grove Park was a breeding ground for crime.

One 17-year-old boy was a trans-sexual prostitute who worked for an escort agency. Another teenager peddled drugs. Newcomers were often led into crime and drugs by hardened teenagers sent there 'as [...]

31

> For most youngsters law-breaking is not a steady occupation, but something that happens sporadically, usually when they are not too busy with their ordinary affairs, when the time and the place and company are propitious [favourable] and a tempting opportunity presents[itself]. Different situations tempt different individuals. Girls may be less prone to housebreaking than boys, but, as experiment has shown, females can be as dishonest as males when presented with a chance to steal small sums covertly. (DJ West, *Delinquency: Its Roots, Careers and Prospects*, 1982.)

In the USA, where over 25 million Americans keep a gun in their homes, it is much easier to obtain firearms than in most other countries. Crime among young people has a far greater element of danger than in countries where guns are not so freely available.

Above *For most young offenders, breaking the law is not a regular occurrence, but is usually done on the spur of the moment, when an opportunity arises.*

> In the city of Detroit, where there are more guns than people, 365 children under the age of sixteen were shot in quarrels during 1986. Forty-three of these died, adding their quota to the city's total of over 600 murders a year. Most of these shootings resulted from arguments over trivial insults – schoolboy bullying takes on a whole new dimension when guns are substituted for fist fights. (JHH Gaute and Robin Odell, *The New Murderers Who's Who*, 1989.)

Recently, some studies have suggested that violent behaviour in young people might be linked to poor diet.

> The Full Circle Residential Research and Treatment Centre, a programme in California, studied seven delinquents referred from juvenile halls, selected on the basis of evidence of learning disabilities and behavior problems that precluded [prevented] their placement in any other therapeutic [curative] programme. In six of the seven, severe behavioral responses resulting from food allergies were discovered, and all seven showed evidence of hypoglycaemia. Six of the children improved markedly in behavior as a result of diet therapy. (Paul A Strasburg, *Violent Delinquents*, 1978.)

Above *The occasional 'junk food' snack does little harm, but some studies have shown that consistently poor diet may be linked to violence among young people.*

Left *Youth crime is a serious problem in New York City, USA. This is a selection of weapons confiscated from pupils in New York's schools.*

Two young offenders work at a special resource centre, learning skills that may be of use to them in daily life. This type of treatment is thought by many to be particularly effective in encouraging young people to steer clear of crime.

While some criminal behaviour might be explained through lack of vitamins or too many of the wrong chemicals in food, most experts look for other explanations for the high level of crime committed by young people. They find it particularly interesting that the crime statistics show that as young people get older, they are less likely to get into trouble.

> Planning for the treatment of individual offenders needs to take into account the important point that most young delinquents, especially those who have been apprehended no more than once or twice, are never reconvicted again once they reach the age of nineteen or twenty. The study findings suggest that this is not merely the result of improved skill in avoiding detection. The behaviour of delinquents genuinely and spontaneously changes in the direction of increasing social conformity with increasing age. (*Delinquency: Its Roots, Careers and Prospects.*)

Or maybe as people start work they no longer have so much spare time on their hands to drift into trouble. They also have access to more money. Some young people, of course, continue acting criminally into adulthood. It is hard to know what to do with young criminals to encourage them to stop. If they are sent to detention centres for punishment, they will meet other young people who may influence them to continue to act criminally after they are released. If they are not sent to detention centres, they may believe they have 'got off' and can commit crimes again without fear.

1 What punishments do you think would be most appropriate for young criminals?
2 Do you think a policy of punishing every crime would stop young people from committing crimes?

34

7

Political crime

It is impossible to understand crime and the behaviour of criminals without first understanding the nature of law.

Laws are made by human beings to help preserve order in society. They define who owns what and give people a code of acceptable behaviour in their dealings with each other. But laws are also designed to protect the existing legal and political system. This can cause problems if an individual, or a group of people, disagrees with their particular system of government.

When Nelson Mandela was brought to court in 1961 charged with inciting South African workers to strike and leaving South Africa without a valid travel document, he refused to accept that he had any legal or moral duty to obey laws made in a parliament where black people were not represented.

Students in Capetown, South Africa, demonstrate for the release of Nelson Mandela. They claimed that he was a political prisoner; he refused to obey laws made by a parliament that contained no representatives elected by the black population.

Two of the leaders during the Civil Rights Movement in the USA in the early 1960s: Martin Luther King Jr (left) and Malcolm X (right).

> The white man makes all the laws, he drags us before his courts and accuses us, and he sits in judgement over us. In this courtroom I face a white magistrate, I am confronted by a white prosecutor, and I am escorted into the dock by a white orderly. The atmosphere of white domination lurks all around in this courtroom. It reminds that me I am voteless because there is a Parliament in this country that is white-controlled. I am without land because the white minority has taken a lion's share of my country and forced my people to occupy poverty-stricken reserves, over-populated and over-stocked in which we are ravaged by starvation and disease. These courts are not impartial tribunals dispensing justice but instruments used by the white man to punish those among us who clamour for deliverance from white rule. (Nelson Mandela, quoted by Donald Woods, *Biko*, 1979.)

Nelson Mandela believed that laws derived from our rulers are not the only laws. Other laws also exist that come from a different source.

The late civil rights leader Martin Luther King Jr, appealed to a higher law, or natural law, in his 'Letter from Birmingham Jail'.

Freedom fighters or criminals?

The PIRA (Provisional Irish Republican Army) in Ireland and ETA (Euzakadi ta Askatasuna) in Spain adopted tactics very similar to those used by the ANC (African National Congress) in South Africa. All three organizations have used violence, through bombing campaigns and shootings. These are mainly aimed at military targets, although each has occasionally hit at non-military ones, such as shopping centres. All three organizations adopted violence around the same time – in the mid-1960s – and all three are Marxist. At one time or another all three have been called terrorist groups.

In it he argued that there are two types of law, just and unjust, and that it is permissible for people to disobey unjust laws. In the same way as people have a moral responsibility to obey just laws, they also have a moral responsibility to disobey unjust laws. A just law is in accordance with God's moral law, but an unjust law is in conflict with that law. King held the view that an unjust law is not, 'rooted in eternal law and natural law. Any law that uplifts human personality is just. Any law that degrades human personality is unjust.'

The idea that natural law supercedes all other laws is not new. The first known legal document, the *Code of Hammurabi*, written about 1900 BC, acknowledged the existence of natural laws, saying that justice was people's inherent right, which came from supernatural forces rather than by royally bestowed favour.

Many people would agree with this, and could think of laws, either now or in the past, which they believed unjust. Obviously, if they broke such a law they would not consider themselves criminals. Nelson Mandela received three years' imprisonment for inciting a strike and a further two years in jail for travelling without a valid permit or passport, but considered he had committed no crime. However, at a later trial, he went even further. He claimed that the use of violence was justified by natural law if it removed an unjust system of government.

A memorial in Belfast, Northern Ireland, to six members of the Provisional IRA who died in prison on a hunger strike. These men had claimed that, as political prisoners, they had the right to be treated differently from ordinary criminals. They had been convicted for committing acts of terrorism. They said they committed the acts for political reasons – to persuade the British to leave Northern Ireland – and so should have been given political status.

Nelson Mandela and his wife Winnie, outside Victor Verster jail in South Africa on his release. He had been a prisoner for twenty-seven years.

> We felt that without violence there would be no way open to the African people to succeed in their struggle against the principle of white supremacy. All lawful methods of expressing opposition to this principle had been closed by legislation, and we were placed in a position in which we had either to accept a permanent state of inferiority, or to defy the government. We chose to defy the law. We first broke the law in a way which avoided any recourse to violence; when this was legislated against, and the government resorted to a show of force to crush opposition to its policies, only then did we decide to answer violence with violence. (Mandela, quoted in *Biko*.)

Nelson Mandela was sentenced to prison as a criminal, and not released until 1990. His supporters claimed he was a political prisoner, jailed for refusing to obey the laws of an unjust system. They claimed his support for the use of violence to change the system was justified by natural law – the same justification used by many nations for the violence they used legally during 'just' wars, such as the Second World War.

But there is a well known saying: 'One person's terrorist is another's freedom fighter'. Your opinion of whether natural law justifies breaking the law, or using violence, will probably depend on whether you believe an existing system of government is just or unjust.

| I   Do you think natural law can ever justify breaking the law? Could stealing ever be justified by natural law?
| 2   Many people believe Nelson Mandela is a freedom fighter and not a terrorist. But what is the difference between him and leaders of groups such as the PIRA in Ireland or ETA in Spain?

8

Facing the future

> Whether he wrote DOWN WITH BIG BROTHER, or whether he refrained from writing it, made no difference. Whether he went on with the diary, or whether he did not go on with it, made no difference. The Thought Police would get him just the same. He had committed — would still have committed, even if he had never set pen to paper — the essential crime that contained all others in itself. Thoughtcrime, they called it. Thoughtcrime was not a thing that could be concealed for ever. You might dodge successfully for a while, even for years, but sooner or later they were bound to get you.

It was always at night — the arrests invariably happened at night. The sudden jerk out of sleep, the rough hand shaking your shoulder, the lights glaring in your eyes, the ring of hard faces round the bed. In the vast majority of cases there was no trial, no report of the arrest. People simply disappeared, always during the night. Your name was removed from the registers, every record of everything you had ever done was wiped out, your one-time existence was denied and then forgotten. You were abolished, annihilated: vaporized was the usual word. (George Orwell, *1984*, 1949.)

John Hurt as the central character, Winston Smith, in a film version of George Orwell's chilling novel, 1984, written in 1948. It prophesied a society run by Thought Police and headed by a dictator called Big Brother (the face of whom stares out from a poster in the background). In this society, even thinking the 'wrong' thoughts was a crime punishable by death.

Youths smoking crack — an illegal drug — in a slum in the South Bronx district of New York City. Drug-related crime is on the increase in many countries, especially in big cities.

George Orwell wrote his nightmare prophecy of a society run by Big Brother and the Thought Police in 1948. But 1984 has come and gone, and Orwell's vision of a world where even thinking the wrong thoughts was a crime has not yet come to pass.

So what does the future hold? Will crime continue to increase? Or will society as a whole become more law-abiding?

> Almost all those who will be filling the high-risk age categories during the first decade of the twenty-first century have already been born; we know their numbers, and who they are. What they will do is less predictable, but some research suggests they will engage in more and more serious acts of criminal violence than generations in the immediate past. (Wesley K Skogan, 'Social change and the future of violent crime', *Violence in America*, Vol. 1, 1989.)

The people who will be young adults, and so in the age groups where crime is most common, at the turn of the century, are only small children now. But experts worry because they are growing up in situations that seem to make some of them much more likely to become criminals.

> Levels of family abandonment, illegitimacy, divorce, single-adult (usually female-headed) families, teenage mothers, young mothers in the labour force, school dropouts, and the proportion of children living in households below the poverty line, all rose steadily during the 1960s and 1970s. Currently they stand at their highest point in modern US history. For example, about 25 per cent of US children are now living in families headed by single adults, and 22 per cent of young children live below the poverty line. These indicators point to a decreasing quantity of 'parenting', growing family discord and disruption, and decreased adult supervision of youths. These indicators of the extent of family disorganization are strongly related to neighbourhood levels of crime, and national trends in violent crime are linked to such factors as the changing proportion of families with only one adult at home and the divorce rate. ('Social change and the future of violent crime', *Violence in America*, vol 1.)

Police in developing countries often do not have the resources to deal with the new breed of international criminal. Here the Colombian police score a rare success in a raid on the home of a drug trafficker – a castle built on the proceeds of selling crack and cocaine.

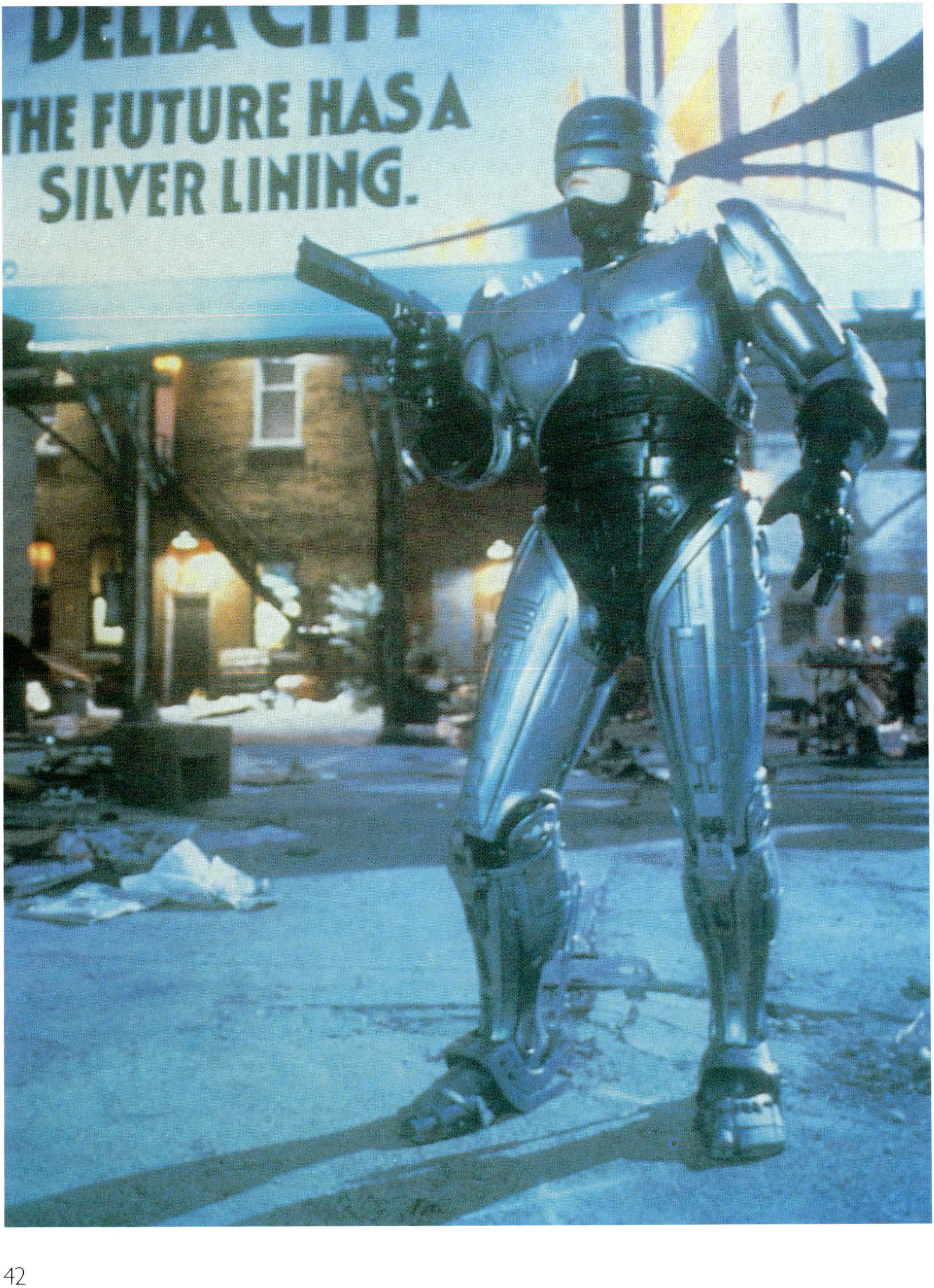
THE FUTURE HAS A
SILVER LINING.

But the future will not only reflect changes in the family structure and the way children are brought up.

> The whole world is undergoing a technological revolution, and crime is adapting just as much as legitimate activity. An explosion in travel has occurred throughout the Western world but nowhere is this more acutely felt than within already crowded Europe. One single example which will illustrate the point is the Netherlands. With a population of about 15 million, they experienced over 200 million border crossings during 1987. The advent of international terrorism and drug trafficking is a development for which our traditional legal systems are poorly prepared. (David A Leonard, 'Policing into the 1990s', *Beyond the Barriers towards 2000* AD.)

Criminals will not be the only ones to benefit from technological advances. The police are already experimenting with new computer-based techniques that make the identification of criminals easier.

Opposite *A futuristic view of law and order; the film* Robocop *featured a police officer who was half-human, half-robot.*

Below *Fingerprinting, long used for identifying criminals, has been turned from a time-consuming task into a fifteen-minute search using a computer system called AFIS (Automated Fingerprint Identification System).*

Professor Alec Jeffreys, who pioneered the technique of 'genetic fingerprinting', shows test results that could be used to tell whether or not a suspect is guilty.

In 1984, Professor Alec Jeffreys discovered a way of identifying people by looking at a thing called DNA, which is stored in the body's cells. These small segments of DNA are dotted about the chromosomes in a pattern so varied that no two people's are alike. They provide a 'genetic fingerprint'.

Professor Jeffreys' technique allows scientists to take a sample of blood or other body fluid found at the scene of a crime, and compare the genetic fingerprint of the criminal with that of likely suspects.

It was first used in Leicester Crown Court in 1986 to show that a 17-year-old accused of murder was actually innocent. He was set free, and the real murderer of three young girls, a man called Colin Pitchfork, was later trapped using the same technique.

> Police arrive at the scene of the crime moments after a young woman is murdered. They dust for fingerprints, but obtain only a partial, smudged impression.

Matching this 'latent' print (an unidentified print obtained at the scene of a crime) with a 'tenprint' (an inked set of fingerprints taken from someone who has previously been arrested and charged with a crime) once required manual searches through thousands of fingerprint cards — a costly, labor-intensive, intimidating task. In fact, manual searches are so difficult that, unless the suspect group can be narrowed, the search for a fingerprint match will not even be attempted.

. . . Today, police can have the name of a suspect in less than 15 minutes with the help of a specialized computer system called an automated fingerprint identification system (AFIS). (Col RL Suthard, 'What is an AFIS?' in *Police Chief*, June 1989.)

The 'smart card' has a silicon chip that can store a great deal of information. However, some people are strongly opposed to the idea of being required to carry any identity card — let alone one with such detailed information on it.

While new information technology may help police to track down criminals, some argue that real advances in fighting crime will only come when everyone carries computerized identity cards.

> Almost every adult in post-industrial societies carries at least one machine-readable identity card, in the form of a cheque or credit card. The rising level of sophisticated crime, the opportunities for major and petty fraud, and the disproportionate effects of terrorism on society now justify the compulsory issue of one more card — a machine-readable national identity card which would also be linked to social security records, making it much quicker and easier to draw benefits from these services.

It now costs very little, about £2, to fit these ID cards, passports, and visa cards with their own microprocessors containing unique personal data (e.g. a digital recording of a fingerprint) to prevent impersonation. As a further precaution, these same data can also be recorded on the appropriate national computer to be activated by the card. Ethically, no innocent person has anything to fear from this system and it will greatly increase his or her own security within the community. It is not a civil right to conceal identity, still less to impersonate someone else. (Richard Clutterbuck, *Terrorism and Guerrilla Warfare*, 1990.)

1   Do you think that every individual should carry an identity card? Do you think this would help cut crime?
2   In George Orwell's *1984*, crime was virtually impossible because of the control Big Brother had over every individual. Is there a danger that the increasing amount of information stored on police computers, and ideas such as identity cards carrying digital records of fingerprints, are leading us towards a *1984* situation?
3   It is technologically possible to take everyone's fingerprints and DNA genetic fingerprint at birth and store the information on computer as part of an individual's birth registration. Given this system's potential for tracking down all types of criminals, why have we not done it? Do you think we should?

45

Glossary

Brutalization The process of becoming unfeeling to the suffering of others through exposure to brutal acts.

Clemency An act of mercy or forgiveness. It is often requested when a death sentence has been passed.

Committed Sent to prison or some other institution, from which you cannot leave without permission.

Compensation The payment of money to make amends for loss or injury sustained through a criminal act.

Delinquent Someone who commits a crime or offence, or acts in an anti-social manner. The word is often used to describe young people (juveniles) who have committed criminal acts.

Deter To prevent crime through the fear of the punishment that will result if you are caught.

Deterrent The punishment that is imposed as the result of a crime. It is imposed with the idea of stopping others committing that crime.

Homicide The killing of one person by another. Deliberate homicide is called murder.

Hypoglycaemia The abnormal reduction of the amount of sugar in the blood.

Jurisdiction The power held by a court or other body.

Justifiable An act that it is possible to show is just or right.

Juvenile A young person aged less than 17.

Juvenile hall A corrective institution for young offenders.

Prerequisite A requirement that must be satisfied before something else can happen.

Prerogative A privilege or power shared by no other. The 'guardian of the Prerogative of Mercy', therefore, is the person with the unique power to grant an act of clemency.

Reformatory A place of correction run with the purpose of persuading its inmates to give up crime.

Rehabilitate To convert a criminal or anti-social person into a citizen ready to be allowed to play a full part in society without restriction.

Reimbursement To pay money of equivalent value to items lost or expenses incurred.

Retribution The repayment of a crime with a punishment.

Slopping out The practice in prison of emptying a bucket which has been left in a cell and used as a toilet.

Status quo The existing state of affairs. Keeping things as they are now.

Further reading

For older readers

Clark, Ramsey, *Crime in America* (Cassell and Co, 1970)

Gaute, JHH and Odell, Robin, *The New Murderers Who's Who* (Harrap Books, 1989)

Leyton, Elliot, *Compulsive Killers: The story of Modern Multiple Killers* (New York University Press, 1986)

Pierrepoint, Albert, *Executioner: Pierrepoint* (George G Harrap, 1974)

Plate, Thomas, *Crime Pays* (Simon and Schuster, 1975)

Wilson, James Q, *Thinking about Crime* (Basic Books, 1975)

Woods, Donald, *Biko* (Penguin Books, 1979)

For younger readers

Edwards, Richard, *Law and Order* (Wayland, 1987)

Gibson, Michael, *Poverty* (Wayland, 1987) and *Unemployment* (Wayland, 1986)

May, Doreen and Pead, David, *Law and Order* (Wayland, 1986)

Picture acknowledgements

The publishers would like to thank the following for providing the illustrations in this book:
The Ancient Art and Architecture collection 4; BFI Stills, Posters and Designs 39; Camera Press *front cover*, 7 (Emile Perauer), 8 (Andrew Varley), 11 (Violette Roch), 16 (Snowdon), 17 (Julian Herbert), 19 (CTK), 24 (Richard Open), 25 (D Baxter), 27 (David Hoffman), 28; Mary Evans13, 20; Eye Ubiquitous 37; Joel Finler 42; John Frost Historical Newspapers 31; Sally and Richard Greenhill 9, 34; Photo Co-op 2 (Abel Lagos), 12 (Ingrid Gavshon), 32 (N. Johnston); Photri 29; Frank Spooner/Gamma 14, 15, 18, 22 (Colmano), 23, 30, 35 & 38 (Eric Bouvet), 43 (Patrick Siccoli), 44 (George de Keerle); Topham Picture Library 33 (bottom), 40, 41; Wayland Picture Library 36 (Associated Press), 37, 45 (Hayward Art Group); Zefa 10, 33 (top).

Index